10108

THE AMERICAN GIRLS

 1764 KAYA, an adventurous Nez Perce girl whose deep love for horses and respect for nature nourish her spirit

1774 FELICITY, a spunky, spritely colonial girl, full of energy and independence

 1824 JOSEFINA, a Hispanic girl whose heart and hopes are as big as the New Mexico sky

 1854 KIRSTEN, a pioneer girl of strength and spirit who settles on the frontier

 1864 ADDY, a courageous girl determined to be free in the midst of the Civil War

 1904 SAMANTHA, a bright Victorian beauty, an orphan raised by her wealthy grandmother

1934 KIT, a clever, resourceful girl facing the Great Depression with spirit and determination

 1944 MOLLY, who schemes and dreams on the home front during World War Two

1934

MEET
Kit

An American Girl

By VALERIE TRIPP

ILLUSTRATIONS WALTER RANE

VIGNETTES SUSAN MCALILEY

American Girl®

Visit our Web site at **americangirl.com**.

Printed in China.
05 06 07 08 09 10 LEO 24 23 22 21 20 19

PICTURE CREDITS
The following individuals and organizations have generously given
permission to reprint images contained in "Looking Back": p.61—AP/Wide World Photos
(milk line); pp. 62–63—© Bettmann/Corbis (men in line); American Stock/Archive Photos
(furniture and couple); J.C. Allen & Son, Inc. (selling eggs); National Archives (train riders);
pp. 64–65—copyright 1978 GM Corp., used with permission of GM Media Archives (cars);
reprinted with permission from Montgomery Ward (radio); © Historical Picture Archive/Corbis
(new things); *People's Popular Monthly*, April 1928 (advertisement); Library of Congress (nervous
investors); pp. 66–67—Mary Evans Picture Library, London (panicked investors); Culver Pictures
(headline); © Bettmann/Corbis (car for sale); *Detroit News*, July 1930, photo courtesy of Archives
of Labor and Urban Affairs, Wayne State University (man holding sign); AP/Wide World Photos
(milk line); courtesy of Great Smoky Mountains National Park (schoolchildren); pp. 68–69—
"The Homeless Shantytown Known as Hooverville," ref. no. 20102, University of Washington
Libraries, James Patrick Lee Collection; Brown Brothers (New York apple sellers); American
Stock/Archive Photos (woman apple seller); Culver Pictures (Burns and Allen); courtesy
Shirley Temple Black and *Photoplay* magazine; FDR Library (campaign advertisement);
© Bettmann/Corbis (Roosevelt supporters).

Cover Background by Mike Wimmer

Library of Congress Cataloging-in-Publication Data

Tripp, Valerie, 1951–
Meet Kit, an American girl / by Valerie Tripp ;
illustrations Walter Rane ; vignettes Susan McAliley.
p. cm. — (The American girls collection)
"Book 1."
First in a series of six books about Kit.
Summary: When her father's business closes and her family
is forced to make changes because of the Great Depression,
nine-year-old Kit responds with resourcefulness.
ISBN 1-58485-016-7 (pbk.). — ISBN 1-58485-017-5 (hc.)
1. Depressions—1929—Juvenile fiction.
[1. Depressions—1929—Fiction. 2. Resourcefulness—Fiction.]
I. Rane, Walter, ill. II. Title. III. Series.
PZ7.T7363 Mdk 2000 [Fic]—dc21 99-088029 CIP AC

FOR MY AUNT, MAXINE HANSEN MARTIN,
WITH ALL MY LOVE

TABLE OF CONTENTS

KIT'S FAMILY
AND FRIENDS

CHAPTER ONE
GOOD NEWS   1

CHAPTER TWO
READ ALL ABOUT IT   14

CHAPTER THREE
IT'S NOT FAIR   30

CHAPTER FOUR
MOTHER'S BRAINSTORM   44

LOOKING BACK   61

SNEAK PEEK   71

KIT'S FAMILY

DAD
*Kit's father, a
businessman facing
the problems of the
Great Depression*

MOTHER
*Kit's mother, who takes
care of her family and
their home with strength and
determination*

KIT
*A clever, resourceful
girl who helps her family
cope with the dark days
of the Depression*

CHARLIE
*Kit's affectionate and
supportive sixteen-
year-old brother*

**UNCLE
HENDRICK**
*Mother's wealthy and
disapproving uncle*

MRS. HOWARD
*Mother's garden club
friend, who is a guest in
the Kittredge home*

**STIRLING
HOWARD**
*Mrs. Howard's son,
whose delicate health
hides surprising
strengths*

**RUTHIE
SMITHENS**
*Kit's best friend, who
is loyal, understanding,
and generous*

GOOD NEWS

Click, clack, clackety!
Kit Kittredge smiled as she typed. She loved the sound the typewriter keys made as they struck the paper and the *ping!* of the bell when she got to the end of a line. She loved the inky smell of the typewriter ribbon, and the way the black letters looked as they marched across the page, telling a story the way *she* wanted it told.

It was a hot afternoon in August. Kit and her best friend Ruthie were in Kit's room writing a newspaper for Kit's dad. Kit was not a very good typist. She used only her two pointer fingers, and she made a lot of mistakes, which she had to xxxxx out. But Dad never minded. Every night when he came home from work, he gave Kit the real newspaper so that she could read the headlines and the baseball scores and the funnies. He was always very pleased when Kit gave him one of her newspapers in return.

Kit finished the paragraph she was typing. "Read me what we have so far," said Ruthie.

Kit cleared her throat and read:

```
    Ruthie Smithens and Kit Kittredge are
reading lots of books this summer.
Ruthie has read the Blue, Yellow, XXX
and Red Fairy Books by Andrew Lang.
She is nowt reading The Lilac Fairy
Book. "I am interested in princes
and princesses, so I like fairy tales,"
ssaid Ruthie. Kit Kittredge is rreading
The Adventures of Robin Hood and His
Merry Men. "I like the way Robin Hood
tricks the bad guy, the Sheriff of
Nottingham," said Kit." And the way he
robs rich people and gives their money
to poor people. I think it would bee
great to live in XXX Sherwood Forest."
```

"That's good," said Ruthie when Kit finished reading. "I like it."

"Me, too," said Kit. "What should we write about now?"

"Write about Charlie and the cookies," said Ruthie. Charlie was Kit's brother, who was sixteen.

Kit thought a moment. Then she typed:

> Congratulations to Charlie Kittredge!
> He et set a World's Record today. He
> ate A a Hole Kwhole plate of gingersnaps
> that were supposed to be fore Mother's
> garden club. Charlie is going to college
> in a few weeks. He should try out for KK
> the Eating Team!

Ruthie looked over Kit's shoulder and giggled as she read what Kit had written. "Now what?" she asked.

Kit picked up a pencil and put it behind her ear so that she'd look like a newspaper reporter. "Well," she said, "we could write about how hot it is."

Ruthie nodded, quickly at first, then slower and slower. Finally she let her chin fall to her chest, closed her eyes, and pretended to snore.

"You're right," said Kit. "Weather's boring. There aren't any *people* in it. This is supposed to be a newspaper, not a *snooze*paper."

3

"You could write about how your mother redecorated your room," Ruthie said. "I think it's as pretty as a princess's room, don't you?"

"Mmm," answered Kit, with a crooked smile. "It's okay. It's just a little too . . . *pink* for me. I'd rather sleep in a tree house, like Robin Hood."

Ruthie shook her head. "You're crazy," she said.

"Yup," said Kit cheerfully. She knew Ruthie was right, of course. Her room *was* pretty. Mother had redecorated it for her earlier that summer as a surprise. And, as with everything Mother did, it was lovely. Kit's room was painted pale pink with white trim. There was a canopy bed as high and white and fluffy as a cloud, and a dressing table with a lacy skirt around it. The desk was white and spindly-legged. It looked too delicate to hold the big black typewriter that crouched on it.

Mother had asked Kit to keep the typewriter in the closet, please, and take it out only when she used it. But Kit always forgot to put the typewriter away. Besides, she used it a lot. The typewriter ended up being on the desk all the time, even though it looked out of place in the frilly room.

Kit squirmed on the poufy stool that had

replaced her old swivel chair. She believed in telling the truth straight-out. But so far she hadn't told Mother that she *felt* as out of place in the frilly room as the typewriter *looked*. Mother was so pleased with all the lacy pinkness, and so sure the room was a girl's dream. *Which it probably is,* Kit admitted to herself, *just not mine.*

"The redecorating story's no good because Dad knows all about it," she said to Ruthie. "It's not new." Kit sighed. "I wish something would happen around here. Some dramatic *change.* Then we'd have a headline that would really grab Dad's attention."

"Like in the real newspapers," said Ruthie.

"Exactly!" said Kit.

"I don't know," said Ruthie. "When my parents read the headlines these days, they get worried. The news is always about the Depression and it's always bad. I don't think we want our paper to be like that."

"No," said Kit. "We want *good* news."

She knew there hadn't been much good news in the real newspapers for a long time. The whole country was in a mess because of the Depression. Dad had explained it to her. About three years ago, people got nervous about their money and stopped

5

buying as many things as they used to, so some stores had to close down. The people who worked in the stores lost their jobs. Then the factories that made  the things the stores used to sell had to close down, so the factory workers lost their jobs, too. Pretty soon the people who'd lost their jobs had no money to pay their doctors or house painters or music teachers, so those people got poorer, too.

Kit was glad that her dad still had his job at his car dealership. She and Ruthie knew kids at school whose fathers had lost their jobs. They'd seen those fathers selling apples on street corners, trying to earn a few cents a day. Some kids had disappeared from school because their families didn't have enough money to pay the rent anymore, and they had to move. Dad said the Depression was like a terrible slippery hole. Once you fell in, it was almost impossible to get out. Kit knew the Depression was getting worse all the time because the newspaper headlines said so almost every night.

But inside Kit's house, no dramatic changes worth a headline seemed to be happening. The girls

6

were about to give up on finding any news—good or bad—when Charlie popped his head in the door.

"Hey, girls," he said. "Mother's garden club's here. You better get downstairs quick if you want anything to eat. I saw Mrs. Culver already diving headfirst into the nut dish."

"Thanks for telling us, Charlie!" said Kit.

"Oh, boy!" said Ruthie. "Maybe there'll be some cake for us!"

"Maybe there'll be some *news* for us!" said Kit. She grabbed her notepad and took the pencil from behind her ear. "Come on!"

Kit and Ruthie thundered down the stairs. They slowed their steps in the hallway so that they wouldn't sound, as Mother always said, like a herd of stampeding elephants. Mother liked things to be *just so* when the garden club ladies came. She brought out all her best crystal, china, silver, and linen and arranged her most beautiful plants on the terrace where the ladies met. Kit could hear the ladies' voices and the clink of their iced tea glasses out on the terrace now.

Above all the other voices, Kit heard Mrs. Wolf complimenting Mother. "Margaret," Mrs. Wolf was saying, "your sponge cake is perfection. Mine is just that—a sponge!" Mrs. Wolf hooted at her own joke before she went on. "Please give me your recipe."

"I'd be glad to," said Mother, just as Kit and Ruthie stepped onto the terrace. Mother looked as cool and slender as a mint leaf in her pale green dress. Kit wanted to fling herself at Mother and hug her. But she held herself back. Her fingers had typewriter ink on them. It would never do to leave ink stains on Mother's perfect green dress!

Mother smiled when she saw the girls. Then she turned to her guests and said, "Ladies, you remember Ruth Ann Smithens and my daughter Kit, don't you?"

"Yes, of course!" said the ladies. "Hello, girls!"

"Hello," said Kit and Ruthie politely.

"Do help yourselves to some refreshments, girls," said Mother.

"We will!" said Kit and Ruthie, smiling broadly.

The girls filled their plates and retreated to a corner behind a potted palm to enjoy their feast and observe the ladies. At first the ladies discussed garden club business, such as how to get rid of bugs, slugs, and other garden pests. It was pretty boring, *phlox*

although the girls did get giggly when
Mrs. Willmore said she was just beside
herself because she had spots on her phlox.

Then the talk moved on to who was going
to weed the flower bed at the hospital, which the
garden club ladies took turns doing.

"I believe it is my turn," said Mrs. Howard.
"But I'm afraid I won't be able to weed this month.
In fact . . ." She hesitated, and blinked her big round
eyes. "I'm afraid I won't be able to be part of the
garden club at all anymore."

Kit and Ruthie looked at each other and raised
their eyebrows. This sounded interesting. Why
would Mrs. Howard be quitting the garden club? Kit
leaned forward so that she could hear better. *There
may be a story in this for our newspaper,* she thought.

All the ladies murmured that they were sorry,
and Mother said, "Oh, Louise! That's too bad!"

"Well," said Mrs. Howard, "I'm moving to
Chicago. My husband is already there, and so
my son Stirling and I are going to join him. He's
pursuing a business opportunity."

"Ahh!" said all the ladies brightly. They all
knew what that meant. Kit did, too. It meant that

There may be a story in this for our newspaper, Kit thought.

Mr. Howard had gone to Chicago to look for a job. Everyone knew that Mr. Howard had not had a job for two years, ever since the company he worked for here in Cincinnati had gone out of business.

"Where will you live in Chicago?" a lady asked.

"I'm not sure yet," said Mrs. Howard, blinking again. "Mr. Howard hasn't settled anywhere. We'll be hither, thither, and yon for a while!"

The ladies smiled, but Kit saw little lines of concern on their faces. The whole thing sounded pretty fishy to Kit. *If the Howards have no place to live in Chicago, why are they leaving their house in Cincinnati?* she wondered. Then suddenly, it dawned on her. The Howards *couldn't* stay in their house. They didn't have enough money anymore. And Mr. Howard didn't have a job or a place for them to live in Chicago, either. That was the truth—Kit was sure of it. She was pretty sure that all the ladies knew it, too, but no one would say it out loud.

There was an awkward silence. Then Mother spoke up and made everything better. "I have a marvelous idea, Louise!" she said to Mrs. Howard. "We'd love it if you and dear Stirling would stay in our guest room until your husband is settled in

11

Chicago and sends for you. Stirling is about Kit's age. I'm sure they'll get along beautifully."

Ruthie nudged Kit, but Kit held her finger to her lips to signal Ruthie not to say anything.

The ladies turned toward Mrs. Howard, waiting anxiously for her answer to Mother's invitation.

"Well," said Mrs. Howard slowly. "If you're *sure* it isn't too much trouble, Stirling and I would love to stay. Thank you, Margaret."

"That's all settled, then," said Mother calmly.

All the ladies brightened up, as if a cloud had blown away. Kit started scribbling notes on her notepad, and Ruthie whispered to her, "Who's this boy Stirling?"

Kit shrugged. "He's Mrs. Howard's son, I guess," she said. "I haven't met him."

"You will," said Ruthie. "He's going to be living in your house."

"Looks like it," said Kit. She liked the idea. Boys were always up to *something*. Stirling was sure to be a good source of stories for her newspaper for Dad. And it would be nice to have a boy around, especially after Charlie left for college. She and Stirling could play catch together. They could talk about the

Cincinnati Reds baseball team, which
Kit loved and Ruthie, quite frankly,
didn't care about. And Stirling could join
in when she and Ruthie acted out stories
from the books they read.

Kit grinned at Ruthie. "When we play Robin
Hood, Stirling can be the Sheriff of Nottingham,"
she said. "Boys like to be the bad guy."

Ruthie had a big bite of cake in her mouth.
She swallowed, then grinned back at Kit. "Well,"
she said. "You never know. Stirling might rather
be Prince Charming and perform good deeds."

"He's already done one good deed," said Kit.

"What?" asked Ruthie.

"Come on," said Kit. "I'll show you."

The two girls slipped back inside the house and
ran up the stairs to Kit's room. Kit stood in front of
the typewriter. "Stirling's given us a headline," she
said to Ruthie. "Look."

Kit typed in capital letters:

THE HOWARDS ARE COMING!

READ ALL ABOUT IT

a kit bag

Kit's real name was Margaret Mildred Kittredge. She was named after her mother and an aunt of her dad's. But when she was very little, her dad used to sing her a song that went like this:

Pack up your troubles in your old kit bag and smile, boys, smile . . .

It was a song he'd learned when he was a soldier fighting in the Great War. Kit loved it. She'd beg Dad, "Sing my song! Sing the kit song!" Pretty soon everyone began to call her Kit, which was also short for Kittredge, and the name stuck. Kit didn't like the name Margaret Mildred anyway. It didn't fit her.

It was too flouncy. Kit was *not* a flouncy girl.

Right now she was feeling especially exasperated with flounces, because the stool she was sitting on was covered with them. Ruthie and the garden club ladies had left, and Kit was finishing her newspaper for Dad. She had to sit with one leg bent under her to reach the typewriter because the new flouncy stool was as soft as a marshmallow and too low.

Kit rolled her newspaper out of the typewriter and read it. She was very pleased with her headline, 'The Howards Are Coming!'

That ought to get Dad's attention! Under the headline, Kit had written:

Mrs. Howard is in Mother's garden club. Mrs. Howard and her son Stirling are going to be staying with the Kittredge family for a wwhile. Mr. Howard is in Chicago. Having the Howards Here will be Fun because Stirling can play catch with Kit Kittredge, thr best nine-year-old catcher in Cincinnati!!

Garden Club Trouble:
Phlox spots put Mrs.
Willmore beside herself!

Kit was struggling with her drawing of two Mrs. Willmores when she heard the car horn's cheery *honk-honk* that signaled her favorite moment of the day. Dad was home from work! Kit snatched up her newspaper, flew downstairs, and burst out the door.

"Extra! Extra! Read all about it!" she shouted, waving her newspaper as Dad climbed out of his car.

Dad caught Kit up in his arms. "How's my girl?" he asked.

"Great!" said Kit when her feet were back on the ground. "Look! I've got a newspaper for you today!"

"Oh ho," said Dad. His blue eyes were twinkly.

He smiled a broad smile as he took Kit's newspaper and handed her the real one. He read Kit's headline in a booming voice. "'The Howards Are Coming!'" Then he glanced at Kit and spoke in his normal voice. "Are they coming for dinner?"

"Nope!" said Kit. "It's better than that! Read the whole story!"

Kit watched as Dad's eyes scanned the story. She noticed, much to her surprise, that his smile faded as he read.

When Dad spoke his voice sounded funny, as if he was trying too hard to be hearty. "Well," he said. "This *is* big news!" He gave Kit's hair a gentle tug. "I'm a lucky guy to have my own personal reporter to keep me on top of all the late-breaking stories," he said. "Come on, sweetheart. Let's go get the details from your mother."

Grownups are funny, Kit thought as she walked along next to Dad. *They don't react the way you expect them to.* Anyone would think that Dad was not pleased to have the Howards coming to stay. But why on earth wouldn't he be?

Two days later, Kit and Ruthie were sitting on the front steps waiting for Stirling and Mrs. Howard to arrive. The girls were reading while they waited. At least, Ruthie was reading. Kit was too distracted. She was really just looking at the pictures in her book.

Kit's copy of *Robin Hood and His Adventures* had belonged to Charlie when he was her age. It had wonderful illustrations, which Kit loved to study. She especially loved reading about the tree houses that Robin and his men lived in. The houses were connected by swinging bridges and catwalks made out of vines. Kit longed to sleep in a tree house high up near the sky, surrounded by leaves. She imagined that at night, stars peeked through the leaves and the wind made the branches sway.

Kit had spent many hours drawing plans for a tree house that she and Ruthie could build. Kit was not very good at sketching. Her drawings always looked like doghouses stuck up in trees. They didn't look anything like the tree houses in Sherwood Forest.

"I bet," said Kit, "that Stirling can help us build a tree house."

"Mmm," said Ruthie, with the tiniest hint of

18

irritation at being interrupted when she was deep into the story of *Beauty and the Beast.*

It was hot, and the girls were licking chunks of ice that had been chipped off the big block of ice in the icebox. Kit had her catcher's mitt next to her, too. She wanted Stirling to see right away that she was interested in books and baseball and was not the type of girl who only cared about things like dusting and baking and dresses.

Kit's ice chunk had melted to a sliver when, at last, a cab pulled up to the end of the driveway. Kit and Ruthie stood up and waited politely on the front steps. The cab door opened, and Mrs. Howard and a boy got out. When she saw Stirling, Kit felt as if someone had dropped her ice chip down her back, she was so surprised.

Ruthie whistled softly. "I thought your mother said that Stirling was about our age," she whispered. "He looks like he's in kindergarten!"

Stirling stood next to the cab on two of the skinniest legs Kit had ever seen. He was short and pale and skinny all over. His head looked too big for his scrawny neck.

19

The screen door opened, and Mother came out of the house. She stood between Kit and Ruthie and put her hands on their shoulders.

"Mother!" whispered Kit indignantly. "Stirling's a shrimp!"

"Now, Kit," said Mother. "Stirling is small for his age because his health is delicate. But I'm sure he's a very pleasant fellow." Gently, she pushed the girls forward. "Come along, ladies," she said. "Let's go greet our guests and make them feel welcome."

Kit and Ruthie and Mother walked down the steps and toward the driveway. Mrs. Howard and the cab driver were unloading boxes and suitcases from the cab. Stirling just stood there.

"Oh!" said Mrs. Howard, all aflutter. "Margaret! You are such a dear to have us!" She turned to Stirling. "Shake hands with Mrs. Kittredge, lamby," she said. "And say hello to Kit and Ruthie."

Stirling shook Mother's hand and nodded at the girls. He looked even worse close-up. He had colorless hair, colorless eyes, and a red, runny nose. Kit towered over him, and Ruthie could have made two of him, he was so puny.

"Oh, dear!" fussed Mrs. Howard. "All this

excitement is not good for Stirling, the poor lamb! He'll have to lie down right away and rest."

"Of course," said Mother. "Come with me and we'll get him settled."

Kit and Ruthie stood on the driveway and watched as Mrs. Howard and Mother propelled Stirling into the house. The cab driver followed them, carrying an armload of suitcases and boxes.

As soon as they were gone, Kit turned to Ruthie and imitated Stirling. She snuffled her nose and made her eyes wide and unblinking.

Ruthie giggled, and then she said, "Of course in fairy tales you always learn not to judge by appearances. Lots of times perfectly nice people are under a spell. Think of *Beauty and the Beast*."

But over the next few days, it was clear to Kit that Ruthie's *Beauty and the Beast* theory didn't work in real life, at least not in Stirling's case. He never said a word. But then, he didn't have to. His mother did all the talking, and most of her sentences began with the words "Stirling can't."

When Kit and Ruthie invited Stirling to run through the sprinkler with them, Mrs. Howard said, "Stirling can't be in the sun because his skin is so fair. And Stirling can't run because he has weak lungs. Stirling can't get wet because he might catch a chill. And Stirling can't play in the yard because he's allergic to bee stings." Kit abandoned any idea of Stirling helping with a tree house or playing catch. Pretty soon, Kit and Ruthie gave up on inviting Stirling to do *anything*, because the answer was always "Stirling can't."

At first, Kit thought Mrs. Howard was making the whole thing up about how fragile Stirling was. It wasn't as if he had a sickness like rickets or scurvy or any of the really interesting diseases Kit knew about from reading pirate stories. Stirling didn't even have any spots or rashes. However, after he'd been there a week, Stirling got truly sick. Though it was only a cold, he did have a fever and a terrible cough. Mrs. Howard said that he had to stay in bed and have all his meals brought to him on a tray.

Kit could hear Stirling coughing and sniffling and blowing his nose all day long. Everyone had to tiptoe past the door to his room so they wouldn't disturb Stirling in case he was napping. Kit held her nose when she passed by, because the hall

 outside his room smelled strongly
of Vicks VapoRub even though
the door was always shut.

But one afternoon, Kit noticed that the door
to the guest room was open. She sneaked a peek
inside. Stirling was propped up on the pillows, and
Mrs. Howard was nowhere to be seen. Of course, it
was hard to see *anything* in the room. It was dark
because the shades were pulled down.

Kit stood in the doorway and looked at
Stirling's moon-white face on the pillow. "Gosh,
it sure is stuffy in here," Kit said to Stirling. "Don't
you want me to open the window or something?"

Stirling nodded.

Kit opened the window a crack so that a breath
of air and a thin line of sunlight came through.
"That's better!" she said. Kit turned to go. She
was halfway to the door when she saw
a photograph next to Stirling's bed that
stopped her in her tracks. "Hey!" she
said. "Is that Ernie Lombardi, the catcher
for the Reds?"

Stirling's round eyes were as unblinking as an
owl's as he looked at Kit. His nose was stuffed up,

so his voice sounded weirdly low and husky. "Schnozz," he croaked.

For a second, Kit didn't understand. Then she laughed and nodded. "Schnozz!" she said. "That's Ernie Lombardi's nickname because he has such a big nose."

In answer, Stirling blew *his* nose, which made a nice honking sound.

Kit laughed again. "Ernie Lombardi is my favorite player on the Cincinnati Reds," she said. "He's the reason I'm a catcher. Well, and because my dad was a star catcher on his college team. Did you know that Ernie's the biggest guy on the Reds?"

"Six foot three," whispered Stirling hoarsely. "Two hundred and thirty pounds."

"Right!" said Kit, delighted. She rattled on. "It's funny that you like him," she said, "because he's so big and you're so little."

"That's why," said Stirling simply. He didn't sound the least bit offended, even though right after she spoke, Kit realized that she'd said something she shouldn't have.

"You know what?" said Kit, suddenly inspired. "I have a newspaper article about Ernie Lombardi.

24

It has a photograph of him holding seven baseballs in one hand at the same time. It used to be tacked up on my wall. My mother wouldn't let me put it back up after my room was painted pink, but I bet I can find it. Want to see it?"

Stirling nodded vigorously, and Kit noticed that his eyes weren't colorless at all. They were gray.

"Okay!" she said. "I'll get the article and you can read all about it!" Kit tore back to her room and rummaged through the drawers of her desk. Where was that newspaper article with the photo of Schnozz? She hoped Mother hadn't thrown it away! Scrambling wildly through the bottom drawer, Kit found the scrap of newspaper at last. She raced back to Stirling's room shouting, "I found it!"

Kit flung open the door and *BAM!* The door hit Mrs. Howard, who was standing right inside with a silver tray in her hands.

"MY LAND!" shrieked Mrs. Howard. She lurched forward and the tray, which had one of Mother's best china teacups and saucers on it, went flying. The hot tea sloshed out all over the rug. The cup hit the floor and shattered, and the tray clanged to the ground with a noise like cymbals.

Kit flung open the door and BAM! The door hit Mrs. Howard,
who was standing right inside with a silver tray in her hands.

"Oh dear, oh *dear!*" fussed Mrs. Howard. At the same time, Stirling started to cough loudly. Kit tried to apologize in a voice louder than his coughs, and Charlie appeared and added to the commotion by asking, "What happened? What's all the noise?"

They were all talking at once when Mother came in. "Good gracious!" she said above all the racket. "*Now* what?"

Everyone stopped talking, even Mrs. Howard.

"Will someone please tell me what is going on?" asked Mother, not sounding at all like her usual serene self.

Everyone looked at Kit.

Kit knew that Mother disliked messes, so she tried to explain how this one was just an accident. "I was coming in here to show Stirling my picture of Ernie Lombardi," she said, "and I didn't know that Mrs. Howard was right behind the door. I was in a hurry and I—"

Mother held up her hand to stop Kit. "Don't tell me," she said. "I can imagine the rest." She shook her head. "How many times have I told you to slow down and watch where you're going, Kit?"

"I'm sorry," said Kit.

Mother stooped down to pick up the broken cup. "Just look at what you've done," she said.

Kit was shocked. It wasn't like Mother to scold her like this. "But it wasn't *my* fault," she protested. "It was an accident. It was *nobody's* fault."

"Nobody's fault," repeated Mother. "And yet look at the mess we are in." She looked up at Kit. "Please go now," she said. "I'll help Mrs. Howard clean up. And Kit, dear, please don't barge in here bothering Stirling and making messes anymore."

"But I didn't—" Kit began.

"That's enough, Kit," said Mother. "Go now."

Kit gave up. She turned on her heel and stormed back to her room. Mother seemed to think that the mess was all her fault, but it *wasn't*! She didn't *mean* to knock into Mrs. Howard. Stupid old Stirling was more to blame for the mess than Kit was. If he weren't sick, his mother wouldn't have been bringing him hot tea in the middle of the afternoon in the first place!

Kit flung herself down at the desk and looked at the wrinkled newspaper article in her hand. What did it matter that her photo of Ernie Lombardi holding seven baseballs was all crumpled up? She couldn't put it up on her new pink walls, and she sure wasn't going to show it to Stirling. She wasn't going to try to be nice to old sniffle-nose Stirling ever again. Look at the trouble it caused her.

Nothing made Kit more angry than being unjustly accused. She didn't mind a good fair fight. But to be blamed for something that was not her fault? That she could not stand. In books when people were accused of crimes they didn't commit, someone like Nancy Drew or Dick Tracy always came around and proved that they were innocent. Kit could see that in her case, she was going to have to speak for herself. She knew just how to do it, too. She'd write a special newspaper for Dad. Then at least *one* person would know her side of the story.

Kit rolled a piece of paper into the typewriter. In capital letters, she typed her headline:

IT'S NOT FAIR

Pounding the typewriter keys as hard as she could made Kit feel better. The good thing about writing was that she got to tell the whole story without anyone interrupting or contradicting her. Kit was pleased with her article when it was finished. It explained exactly what had happened and how the teacup was broken. Then at the end it said:

```
   Sometimes a person is trying to do
something nice for another person and
it turns XXX out sadly badly by mistake.
When ssomething bad happens and it isn't
my anyone's fault, no one should be
blamed. It's not fair!
```

Kit pulled her article out of the typewriter and marched outside to sit on the steps and wait for Dad to come home. She brought her book about Robin Hood to read while she waited.

She had not been reading long before the screen door squeaked open and slammed shut behind her. Kit didn't even lift her eyes off the page.

Charlie sat next to her. "Hi," he said.

Kit didn't answer. She was a little put out with Charlie for adding to the trouble in Stirling's room.

"What's eating you, Squirt?" Charlie asked.

"Nothing," said Kit as huffily as she could.

Charlie looked at the piece of paper next to Kit. "Is that one of your newspapers for Dad?" he asked.

"Yup," said Kit.

Charlie picked up Kit's newspaper and looked at the headline. "'It's Not Fair,'" he read aloud. Then he asked, "What's this all about?"

"It's about how it's wrong to blame people for things that are not their fault," said Kit. "For example, *me*, for the mess this afternoon."

"Aw, come on, Kit," said Charlie. "That's nothing. You shouldn't make such a big deal of it."

"That's easy for *you* to say!" she said.

31

Charlie took a deep breath in and then let it out. "Listen, Kit," he said, in a voice that was suddenly serious, "I wouldn't bother Dad with this newspaper today if I were you."

Kit slammed her book shut and looked sideways at Charlie. "And why not?" she asked.

Charlie glanced over his shoulder to be sure that no one except Kit would hear him. "You know how lots of people have lost their jobs because of the Depression, don't you?" he asked.

"Sure," said Kit. "Like Mr. Howard."

"Well," said Charlie, "yesterday Dad told Mother and me that he's closing down his car dealership and going out of business."

"*What*?" said Kit. She was horrified. "But . . ." she sputtered. "But *why*?"

"Why do you think?" said Charlie. "Because nobody has money to buy a car anymore. They haven't for a long time now."

"Well how come Dad didn't say anything before this?" Kit asked.

"He didn't want us to worry," said Charlie. "And he kept hoping things would get better if he just hung on. He didn't even fire any of his

"I wouldn't bother Dad with this newspaper today if I were you," said Charlie.

salesmen. He used his own savings to keep paying their salaries."

"What's Dad going to do now?" asked Kit.

"I don't know," said Charlie. "He even has to give back his own car. He can't afford it anymore. I guess he'll look for another job, though that's pretty hopeless these days."

Kit was sure that Charlie was wrong. "Anyone can see that Dad's smart and hardworking!" she said. "And he has so many friends! People still remember him from when he was a baseball star in college. Plenty of people will be glad to hire him!"

Charlie shrugged. "There just aren't any jobs to be had. Why do you think people are going away?"

"Dad's not going to leave like Mr. Howard did!" said Kit, struck by that terrible thought. Then she was struck by another terrible thought. "We're not going to lose our house like the Howards, are we?"

"I don't know," said Charlie again.

Kit could hardly breathe.

"It'll be a struggle to keep it," said Charlie. "Dad told me that he and Mother don't own the house completely. They borrowed money from the bank to buy it, and they have to pay the bank back a little every month. It's called a mortgage. If they don't have enough money to pay the mortgage, the bank can take the house back."

"Well, the people at the bank won't just kick us out onto the street, will they?" asked Kit.

"Yes," said Charlie. "That's exactly what they'll do. You've seen those pictures in the newspapers of whole families and all their belongings out on the street with nowhere to go."

"That is not going to happen to us," said Kit fiercely. "It's *not*."

"I hope not," said Charlie.

"Listen," said Kit. "How come Dad told Mother and *you* about losing his job, but not *me*?"

Charlie sighed a huge, sad sigh. "Dad told me," he said slowly, "because it means that I won't be able to go to college."

"Oh, Charlie!" wailed Kit, full of sympathy and misery. She knew that Charlie had been looking forward to college so much! And now he couldn't go. "That's terrible! That's awful! It's not *fair*."

Charlie grinned a cheerless grin and tapped one finger on Kit's newspaper. "That's your headline, isn't it?" he said. "These days a lot of things happen that aren't fair. There's no one to blame, and there's nothing that can be done about it." Charlie's voice sounded tired, as if he'd grown old all of a sudden. "You better get used to it, Kit. Life's not like books. There's no bad guy, and sometimes there's no happily ever after, either."

At that moment, Kit felt an odd sensation. Things were happening so fast! It was as if a match had been struck inside her and a little flame was lit, burning like anger, flickering like fear. "Charlie," she asked. "What's going to happen to us?"

"I don't know," said Charlie. He stood up to go.

"Wait," said Kit. "How come you told me about Dad? Was it just to stop me from bothering Dad with my newspaper?"

"No," said Charlie. "No. I told you because . . ." He paused. "Because you're part of this family, and I figured you deserve to know."

"Thanks, Charlie," said Kit. She was grateful to Charlie for treating her like a grownup. "I'm glad you told me," she said, "even though I wish none of it were true."

"Me, too," said Charlie. "Me, too."

After Charlie left, Kit sat on the step thinking.
No wonder Dad had not been happy about the
Howards coming to stay. He must have been
worried about more mouths to feed. And no wonder
Mother had been short-tempered today. When she
said that even though it was nobody's fault, they
were still in a mess, she must have been thinking
of Dad. It wasn't his fault that they'd fallen into the
terrible, slippery hole of the Depression, and yet, and
yet . . . it surely seemed as though they had. Just like
the Howards. Just like the kids at school. Just like
the people she'd read about in the newspaper.

The sun was setting, but it was still very hot
outside. The air was so humid, the whole world
looked blurry. Then, all too clearly, Kit saw a terrible
sight. It was Dad. He was walking home. He did not
see Kit yet, but she could see that he looked hot and
tired. There was a discouraged droop to his shoulders
that Kit had never seen before. It made Kit's heart
twist with sorrow. For just the tiniest second, she did
not want to face Dad. She knew that when she did,
she'd have to face the truth of all that Charlie had told

her. But then Kit stood up and straightened her shoulders. Everything else in the whole world might change for Dad, but she wouldn't.

Kit ran to Dad the way she had done every other night of her life when he came home. Dad caught her up and swung her around.

When he put her down, Kit looked Dad straight in the eye. "Charlie told me," she said. "Is it true?"

Dad knelt down so that his eyes were level with Kit's. "Yes," he said. "It is."

"Are we going to be all right?" Kit asked.

"I don't know," said Dad. "I truly don't know."

Kit threw her arms around Dad and hugged him hard. She crumpled up her newspaper in her fist behind Dad's back. Her complaints about Stirling and the teacup seemed silly and babyish now. Charlie was right. Dad didn't need to read her newspaper. Dad knew all about trying to be nice to people and having it turn out badly. He knew all about having bad things happen that were nobody's fault. He knew all about things that were not fair.

❧

38

Kit was a practical girl. She thought it was a waste of time to worry about a problem when you could be *doing* something to solve it. But her family had never had a problem as serious as this one before. All night long Kit lay awake thinking, listening to Stirling cough—and worrying.

The night was very hot. Kit kicked her sheet off and turned her pillow over time and time again because it got sweaty so fast. Finally, Kit got up. It always made her feel better to write. She took her notepad and a pencil out of her desk and sat at the window in the moonlight. She decided to make a list of all the ways she could save the family some money.

> *No dancing lessons*
> *No fancy dresses for dancing lessons*

Kit looked at her list and scolded herself. It was all very well to give up dancing lessons and fancy dresses. Those were things she didn't want. But how about things she *did* want? Kit looked out the window. Then, sadly, she added to her list.

No lumber for a tree house
No new books
No tickets to baseball games
No sweets

There! thought Kit. *I'll show Dad my list tomorrow.*

But by the time Kit went downstairs to breakfast the next morning, Dad had already left.

"He's gone to meet a business friend," said Mother.

"It'd be great if his friend offered Dad a job, wouldn't it?" said Kit.

"Yes," said Mother. "It would." She smiled, but it wasn't one of her *real* smiles.

Kit felt all restless and jumpy. She wanted to be alone so that she could think and work on her list some more. She wandered around the yard for a while before she found a good hideaway under the back porch. *No one will find me here,* she thought.

But she had not been hidden long before Ruthie crawled in next to her.

"How do you always find me?" asked Kit.

Ruthie shrugged. "It's easy," she said. "I just think where I'd be if I were you, and that's where you are. Why are you hiding, by the way?"

"My dad lost his job," said Kit.

"Oh," said Ruthie softly. "That's too bad. I'm sorry." The girls sat together in silence for a minute. That was a good thing about Ruthie. She'd sit and think with Kit. She didn't need to talk all the time. "What are you going to do?" Ruthie asked at last.

Kit handed Ruthie her list. "These are ways I can help save money," she said.

Ruthie read the list. "These are good," she said. "These'll help." But her voice sounded doubtful.

Kit sighed. "The truth is, I've just never given money much thought before," she said.

"I know," said Ruthie. "Me neither."

Kit understood that when Dad sold a car, people gave him money. Dad gave some of the money to Mother. She used it to buy food and clothes and to pay the electric bill and the iceman and to get things for the house. Once a month, Dad paid the bank twenty-five dollars, which, as Charlie had explained, was part of the money that Dad and Mother owed the bank because they'd borrowed it when they bought the house. If there was any money left over after everything was paid, Dad put it in his savings account at the bank.

"Without Dad's job," said Kit to Ruthie, "there won't be any more money coming in. And Charlie said that Dad used up most of his savings to pay his salesmen as long as he could, so soon there won't be any money left in his savings. What'll we do then?"

"I've read lots of books about people who have no money," said Ruthie.

"Me, too," said Kit. "But most of them lived in the olden days on farms or in a forest where they could at least get nuts and berries. We live in modern times in Cincinnati. How will we get food when our money is gone? Will we move to a farm?"

"I don't think your mother would like that," said Ruthie.

"No," sighed Kit. "Besides, none of us knows anything about farming."

Ruthie scratched her knee. "I think," she said slowly, "we're going to have to hope that your dad gets another job."

"Yup," said Kit. "Maybe today." She looked at Ruthie. "What a great headline *that* would be!"

MOTHER'S BRAINSTORM

But Dad didn't get a job that day, or the day after that, or the day after that, though he certainly seemed to be trying. Every day he put on a good suit and rode the streetcar downtown. Every day he said he was going to have lunch with a friend or a business acquaintance. Every day, Kit hoped he'd come home with the good news of a new job. But every afternoon, Dad came home tired and discouraged. All the bad news in the newspapers seemed to be about Kit's own life now.

One afternoon after a week had passed, Kit and Mother were on the back porch shelling peas when a huge black car pulled up in the driveway.

"Oh, no," sighed Mother.

Kit asked, "Is it Uncle Hendrick?"

Mother nodded. She took off her apron and handed it and the peas to Kit. "Quick," she said. "Take these into the kitchen. And Kit, dear, while you're in there, pour us some iced tea and bring it to the terrace." Mother smoothed her hair, adjusted her smile, and walked gracefully toward the car.

Kit was glad to escape inside. Uncle Hendrick was her mother's uncle and the oldest relative Mother had left. He was tall and gray, and he lived in a tall, gray house near downtown Cincinnati. He always seemed to be in a bad mood, like Grandfather in the *Heidi* book before Heidi made him nice. *The last thing Uncle Hendrick needs is lemon,* Kit thought as she put a slice in his glass. *He's already a sourpuss.*

Kit put the iced tea on a tray and carried it to the terrace. Mother was sitting on a wicker chair, but Uncle Hendrick was pacing back and forth. When he saw Kit, he stopped.

Here it comes, thought Kit.

Without even saying hello, Uncle Hendrick barked at Kit, "What's the capital of North Dakota?"

"Bismarck," answered Kit. She was used to such questions from Uncle Hendrick. If he wasn't asking her about capitals, he was asking her multiplication facts. Worst of all were his word problems. "I have two bushels of Brussels sprouts I'm selling for five cents a peck," he said now. "How much do you pay me?"

Kit put the tray on the table to gain some time. She could never keep bushels and pecks straight. *And who wants two bushels of Brussels sprouts anyway?* she thought. "Um, fifty cents?" she guessed.

"Wrong!" said Uncle Hendrick. "You may go."

Mother gave Kit a sympathetic look. But Kit felt sorrier for Mother than she did for herself. She went inside, but she stayed in the dining room where she could hear everything they said.

"Margaret," Uncle Hendrick sighed. "Didn't I tell you and Jack what a mistake it was to sink all your money into that car dealership? If you two had listened to me, you would not be in the fix you are in now. And don't expect me to help you. I won't throw good money after bad."

"We'll be all right, Uncle," said Mother. "I'm sure Jack will find a job soon."

"Humph!" snorted Uncle Hendrick. "No, he will not. Not him. And not during these hard times."

Kit realized that her fists were clenched. Oooh! She wanted to run out onto the terrace and punch Uncle Hendrick. She hated it when he spoke about Dad that way. But Mother didn't say anything.

"And what will you do in the meantime?" Uncle Hendrick continued. "You should sell this house right away, though who'd buy it I can't imagine. Such foolish extravagance to buy it in the first place! You must owe the bank thousands of dollars."

"This is our home, Uncle," Kit heard Mother say. "We'll do whatever we can to keep it."

"Indeed!" said Uncle Hendrick. "And what might that be, if I may ask?"

Mother didn't answer.

"Just as I thought," said Uncle Hendrick smugly. "You haven't any idea. There's nothing you can do."

"Well," said Mother, "we could . . . take in boarders. Paying guests."

Kit felt as surprised as Uncle Hendrick sounded. "Boarders?" he gasped.

"Yes," said Mother. "It's perfectly respectable. We'll take in teachers, or nurses from the hospital."

Gosh! thought Kit. *Would you listen to Mother!*

But Uncle Hendrick had evidently heard enough. "Well, Margaret," he said. "All I can say is that if my sister, your dear mother, could see you now, it would break her heart." With that, Uncle Hendrick strode back to his car and drove away.

Kit ventured out onto the terrace. "Are we really going to take in boarders?" she asked Mother.

Mother smiled, and this time it was one of her real smiles that made Kit feel like smiling, too. "I surprised myself by saying that," said Mother. "I'm afraid I just wanted to shock Uncle Hendrick. But I rather like the idea." Mother laughed. "Yes," she said. "I like the idea a lot. It was a brainstorm."

"What's Dad going to say?" asked Kit.

"That," said Mother, "is a good question."

Kit was not at all sure that she liked Mother's brainstorm. She wasn't crazy about the idea of strangers living in their house, especially considering the way Stirling had turned out.

Kit could tell that Dad didn't like the idea either. Mother had first presented the idea to him in private, of course, before she spoke about it again at dinner that evening. Mrs. Howard was serving Stirling his dinner up in their room, so only the family was at the table.

"We have plenty of room," said Mother. "We should put it to use."

"I don't think it's necessary," said Dad. "I'm making every effort to find a job. Meanwhile—"

"Meanwhile this'll be a way for us to earn some money," said Mother.

Dad sighed. "I hate the idea of you waiting on other people, especially in our own home."

"We'll all chip in to help," answered Mother, in a way that made it clear that the question of taking in boarders was settled. Kit wasn't surprised. There was never any way to stop Mother once she'd made up her mind.

"But where will the boarders stay?" asked Kit.

"Charlie can move to the sleeping porch," said Mother, "and we can put someone in his room."

"It's okay with me," said Charlie with a shrug.

"Thank you, dear," said Mother. "I'm also planning to find two schoolteachers or nurses to share the guest room."

Kit perked up. "Does that mean that Stirling and his mother will be leaving?" she asked. That'd be *one* good thing about Mother's plan at least!

"They'll stay," said Mother. "They'll be paying guests from now on."

"But *where* will they stay?" asked Kit.

Mother looked at Kit and said calmly, "Stirling and his mother will move into your room."

"*Mine?*" asked Kit, in a shocked, squeaky voice.

"Yes," said Mother. "We need them. They've got to stay if we want to make enough money to pay the mortgage every month. I figured it out."

"But Mother!" exclaimed Kit. "Where will *I* sleep?"

"I was thinking," said Mother briskly, "that you could move up to the attic. There's plenty of room up there."

The attic! thought Kit indignantly. She was being exiled to the hot, stuffy attic so that sniffle-nose Stirling could move into *her* room with his hankies and his meals on trays and his Vicks VapoRub!

Oh, oh, *oh!* In Kit's mind she saw her headline again, in letters that were four inches tall:

"It's Not Fair!"

"But Kit," panted Ruthie, out of breath from climbing the stairs up to the attic, "you don't even like your room that much."

It was the next day. Kit and Ruthie were inspecting the attic. It smelled of mothballs, and it was gloomy because the windows were so dusty that the sun couldn't shine through them.

"You told me your room is too pink," Ruthie said. "Why are you so mad about moving out of it?"

"Because it was mine!" said Kit, knowing she sounded peevish. The fact that Ruthie was right, of course, just made Kit madder. "That room belonged to *me*, always, ever since I was a baby. And it just kills me to think that Stirling gets to have it. Why didn't *he* have to move up here?"

"I guess because his mother is paying rent now," said Ruthie calmly. She looked around. "It's not so bad up here," she said. "It's like the attic that Sara Crewe had to move into after she lost all her money. You know, in *The Little Princess*."

Kit felt very impatient with Ruthie and her princesses this morning! "Sara Crewe's room was transformed for her by that Indian guy," Kit said crossly. "Remember? He made it beautiful. He was practically magic about it."

"Your mother's practically magic about making things beautiful, too," said Ruthie. "She'll help you up here, right?"

"Right!" said Kit. But she was dead wrong.

That afternoon, while she was helping Mother make the beds, Kit asked her how they were going to fix up the attic.

Mother said, "I don't have time to help you right now, dear. I'm far too busy getting the rooms ready for the boarders." Mother's arms were full of sheets for the roll-away cot, which was being moved into Kit's old room for Stirling to sleep on. "After you help me, why don't you just poke around up there?" she said. "See what you can find."

Mother spoke in such a distracted manner that Kit's feelings were hurt. Mother had been *so* particular about every detail in Kit's pink room. But she didn't seem to give a hoot about Kit's attic.

Kit climbed slowly up the stairs to the attic. She stood in the middle of the room and looked around at the lumpy, dusty piles that surrounded her. In a far corner, she saw her old brown desk chair. She

saw her old desk, too, hidden under a bumpy
mattress and some boxes. Kit knelt next to
one of the boxes and looked inside. *Now,
if I were in a book,* Kit thought, *I'd find
something wonderful in here.* But the box
had only junk in it: a broken camera, a
pair of binoculars and a compass that must have
belonged to Dad in the war, a gooseneck lamp,
and an old telephone, the kind that looked like
a daffodil. *Old and useless,* thought Kit.

She took the compass out of the box and
hung it around her neck. Then she sank down
to the floor, overwhelmed by sadness. When
she'd been wishing for change so that she could
have a dramatic headline, she'd never imagined
this! Terrible changes! And so many! And so fast!
Dad had lost his job. She had lost her room. And
in a way, they *were* going to lose their house.
They'd still be living in it, but it wouldn't be the
same when it was filled up with strangers. Nothing
would *ever* be the same.

Kit almost never cried. She bit her lip now and
fought back tears. Then, suddenly, Stirling's head
appeared at the top of the stairs.

"What are you doing out of bed?" Kit asked, roughly brushing away a tear.

Kit could tell that Stirling knew she'd been crying, but all he said was, "I'm bringing this stuff from your room." He came all the way up the stairs and handed Kit a box. She noticed that the photo of Ernie Lombardi, wrinkled but smoothed flat, was on top.

"Thanks," said Kit.

"I brought you a tack, too," said Stirling. He gave Kit the tack and looked around. "I guess you can put Ernie Lombardi up anywhere you want to up here, can't you?" he said in his weirdly husky voice. Then he disappeared down the stairs.

After Stirling left, Kit looked down at the photograph. She felt oddly cheered to see it. *Old sniffle-nose Stirling is right,* she thought. *I guess I can put anything anywhere I want up here.*

Kit looked around the long, narrow attic. The ceiling was steeply pitched. There were regular windows at each end of the room, and dormer windows that jutted out of the roof and made little pointy-roofed alcoves, each one about as wide as Kit was tall. The windows went almost all the way to the floor of the alcoves. Kit managed to open one of

*Old sniffle-nose Stirling is right, Kit thought. I guess
I can put anything anywhere I want up here.*

the heavy windows. She knelt down, stuck her head out, and came face-to-face with a leafy tree branch.

At that moment, Kit got a funny excited feeling. Suddenly, she knew exactly what she wanted to do.

Over the next few days, Kit was glad that no one seemed to care what she was up to up in the attic. When she wasn't helping Mother downstairs, she hauled buckets of soapy water up there and scrubbed the windows till they sparkled. She swept the floor and pushed the boxes far to one end of the room. She had decided to use only half of the attic to live in and to pile junk in the other half. Finally the cleaning was done, and the fun part began.

In one alcove, Kit put her rolltop desk and her swivel chair. She put the gooseneck lamp on the desk, along with the telephone, the camera, and her typewriter. That was her newspaper office alcove.

In another alcove, Kit tacked up her photo of Ernie Lombardi. On a nail, she hung her catcher's mitt and the old binoculars. She figured she might need the binoculars if she ever went to a Reds game. That was her baseball alcove.

In the third alcove, Kit made bookshelves out of boards and arranged all her books on them. She found a huge chair that was losing its stuffing, and she shoved it into the alcove and softened it with a pillow. That was her reading alcove.

The last alcove was Kit's favorite. She put the lumpy mattress on an old bed frame and pushed the bed into the alcove with the pillow near the window. She surrounded the bed with some of Mother's potted plants. That was her tree house alcove.

The very first night Kit slept in her tree house alcove, Mother came up to tuck her in. She sat on the edge of Kit's bed, and looked around the attic. Kit watched Mother's face carefully. She knew the attic was a far cry from Mother's idea of what a girl's room should look like.

"Well!" said Mother at last. "A place for every interest and every interest in its place. I can see that you've worked hard to make this attic your room. I'm proud of you, Kit."

"Thanks," said Kit.

"I'm sorry I haven't had time to help you," said Mother. "I'm afraid I've left you all on your own."

"That's okay," said Kit.

Mother kissed Kit's forehead. Then she picked up Kit's book. "Still reading *Robin Hood*?" she asked.

"Yup," said Kit. "*Robin Hood* gave me the idea to make a tree house alcove to sleep in." Kit also had plans for a swinging bridge to connect the window ledge to the tree just outside the window, but she didn't tell Mother. It was going to be a secret escape, like Robin Hood had.

"Good old Robin Hood," said Mother. "Robbing the rich to give to the poor."

Kit propped herself up on her elbows and looked at Mother. "Too bad there isn't any Robin Hood today," she said. "If rich people had to give some of their money to the poor, it would make the Depression better."

"It would help," said Mother. "But I don't think it would end the Depression."

"What will?" asked Kit.

"I don't know," said Mother. "Lots of things, I suppose. People will have to work hard. Use what they have. Face challenges. Stay hopeful." She looked around Kit's attic and smiled. "I guess they'll have to do sort of what you've done up here in your attic. They'll have to make changes and realize that changes can be good." Then she kissed Kit again. "Good night, dear," she said. "Don't read too late."

"I won't," said Kit. "Good night."

After Mother went downstairs, Kit flipped over onto her stomach and looked out the open window. She could hear the leaves rustling outside and see stars peeking through the branches. *'Changes Can Be Good,'* she thought. *That sounds like a headline to me.*

LOOKING BACK

AMERICA
IN
1934

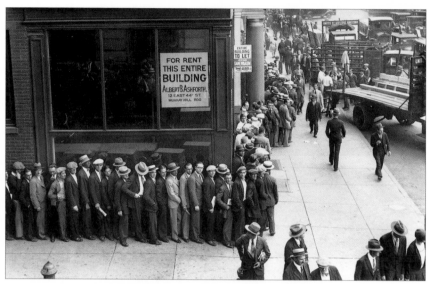

*Long lines of people looking for work or waiting for
a meal were common during the Depression.*

When Kit's father closed his business, the Kittredges
found themselves facing hard times that were shared by
millions of Americans. In 1929, America had fallen into
a financial crisis so serious that it came to be known as
the *Great Depression*. Businesses and banks all across the
country had to close for lack of money. People lost their
jobs and sometimes their life's savings. Families often had
no way to pay for the things they needed to live, such as
groceries and rent.

*Some people
couldn't afford to
keep their homes
and were thrown
out on the streets.*

People found creative ways to cope with the hard times. They planted gardens and raised animals for food, recycled everything they could, and made things they couldn't afford to buy. To save money, many families moved in together.

Families who kept chickens made money by selling eggs.

Others turned their homes into boarding houses, as Kit's family did. But as the Depression deepened, many people ended up homeless and started wandering America in search of food and jobs.

To find work, many people traveled the country by hopping onto slow-moving trains—a dangerous and illegal thing to do. Sometimes whole families "rode the rails" together.

There had been depressions in America's past, but none was as widespread and long-lasting as the Great Depression. Although the start of the Great Depression in 1929 took many Americans by surprise, the causes had been building for many years.

63

Car sales soared in the 1920s, when mass production brought prices down and made more cars available.

By the end of the 1920s, nearly every American home had a radio.

The 1920s had been good years for American business. World War One, the Great War, ended in 1918, and American companies switched from making war supplies to making things like radios, toasters, and cars. Americans supported business growth by buying stock in the companies making these and other goods. A *stock* is a share of a company, and the *stock market* is a system in which people buy and sell shares. The stock market is an important measure of the health of America's financial system, or *economy*. People invest in stocks when they have confidence in the economy and believe they'll make money.

*People who bought stock in a company often received a **stock certificate** showing the number of shares they owned.*

In the 1920s, some people had a lot of money to spend on new clothes, cars, and pastimes.

For a time in the 1920s, stock values went up and people *did* make lots of money. But some investors bought more stock than they could afford. They bought stock on *credit*, or with borrowed money. They believed their stock would increase in value. They planned to repay their loans when they sold their stock at a higher price.

But the economy was getting out of balance as it grew. Business owners and investors were making huge profits, but the wages of working people didn't rise very fast. Many people went into debt buying everyday things on credit. Farmers were already in debt from years of struggling with drought and low crop prices.

Advertisements encouraged people to buy on credit.

As people's debt grew, they stopped buying new things. Companies lost money, so they laid off workers—and then even fewer people could afford new things. Stocks were worth less and less. Confidence in the economy fell. Investors began to sell their stocks, but soon the stocks were worth so little that no one wanted to buy them.

People with money in the stock market grew nervous over news of the drop in stock prices.

65

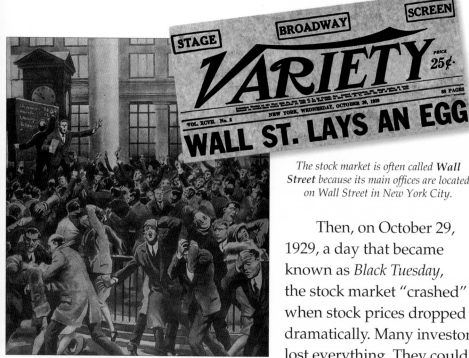

STAGE BROADWAY SCREEN

VARIETY PRICE 25¢.

88 PAGES

VOL. XCVII. No. 3 NEW YORK, WEDNESDAY, OCTOBER 30, 1929

WALL ST. LAYS AN EGG

*The stock market is often called **Wall Street** because its main offices are located on Wall Street in New York City.*

Investors panicked when stock prices fell.

Then, on October 29, 1929, a day that became known as *Black Tuesday*, the stock market "crashed" when stock prices dropped dramatically. Many investors lost everything. They could not pay back the money they had borrowed to buy stocks. The banks that had loaned them money lost everything, too. Within weeks, the entire country started to suffer as businesses and banks shut down and more and more people lost their jobs.

Almost overnight, families who had been comfortable found themselves with nothing. When a bank closed, people were sometimes left with only the money they had at home. Even

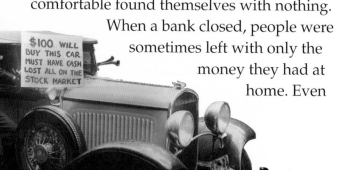

$100 WILL
BUY THIS CAR
MUST HAVE CASH
LOST ALL ON THE
STOCK MARKET

WORK-IS-WHAT-I
WANT-AND-NOT-CHARITY
WHO-WILL-HELP-ME-
GET-A-JOB-7-YEARS-
IN-DETROIT·NO-MONEY
SENT-AWAY·FURNISH·
BEST-OF-REFERENCES
PHONE RANDOLPH 8395 ROOM
#59.

Many people had to rely on charity for basic necessities, such as bread and milk.

children who had put their pennies and nickels into school-sponsored savings programs lost their money. Many people had nowhere to turn for help and were deeply ashamed to go "on relief" or to accept free meals in soup kitchens run by charities. For most, it was the first time they had to rely on charity. But with so many people in need, the charities soon ran out of money, too. Families and neighbors helped one another as much as they could, but often there was not enough to go around.

Like the Kittredges, some families did all right during the first few years of the Depression, but few escaped the hard times entirely. Many children suffered. One West Virginia teacher noticed a student having trouble paying attention during class. When the girl didn't eat at lunchtime, the teacher suggested that the girl run home to get her lunch. She couldn't, the girl replied, because it was Tuesday— her sister's day to eat.

Children who didn't have enough to eat found it hard to stay awake in school.

Homeless people built rough shacks for shelter. Angry Americans called these communities "Hoovervilles" after President Hoover, who appeared to do nothing to end the Depression.

President Herbert Hoover did little to provide leadership or government help. He believed that business, if left alone, would correct itself and the Depression would end. But as the hard times got worse, many Americans lost confidence in the president and in the government.

In the fall of 1930, the International Apple Shippers Association tried to help unemployed workers by selling them apples at $1.75 a crate. By selling the apples for five cents each, a seller could make a $1.85 profit. Thousands of unemployed workers turned to apple selling. Within weeks, however, the supply of apples ran out—and so did the jobs.

By early November 1930, there were 6,000 apple sellers on the streets of New York City.

68

Radio stars George Burns and Gracie Allen

Shirley Temple made her acting debut in 1931 at age three and soon became a movie star.

During the Depression, people looked for ways to forget their troubles. Many homes had radios, and families gathered to listen to the adventures of Little Orphan Annie and Buck Rogers or to the comedy team of George Burns and Gracie Allen. Movie theaters started offering all-day shows for a nickel, and they were soon filled with people trying to escape reality by watching Cary Grant, Jean Harlow, and Greta Garbo on the screen.

The year 1932, when Kit's story begins, was the lowest point of the Great Depression, but no one knew it at the time. Unemployment was at an all-time high, and the future looked bleak. In November, Franklin Delano Roosevelt would be elected president, beating Hoover by a land-slide. Americans were desperate for a change, and they hoped that the new president would lead them out of the Depression.

Many Americans supported Roosevelt, but others believed he would ruin the country.

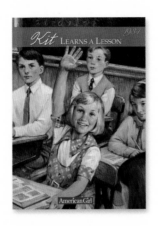

A SNEAK PEEK AT

Kit
LEARNS A LESSON

*When a boy at school teases Kit, she decides
to get revenge!*

A few days later, Kit's class was on the stage in the school auditorium working on the backdrop for the Thanksgiving pageant. Stirling had drawn the outline on big sheets of paper that were pinned to the curtains at the back of the stage. The boys were painting in the fruits and vegetables. The girls were cutting out paper turkey feathers. Stirling was standing on a stool, gluing the finished feathers onto the outlines of the giant turkeys.

Mr. Fisher was far away, up in the balcony wrestling with the spotlights, and Roger was taking advantage of his absence by being a general pain.

He came over and jabbed Stirling with his paintbrush. "So, Stirling," he said, "when's the wedding for you and Kit?"

It was as if Stirling hadn't heard Roger. He stepped down off his stool and calmly began brushing glue onto another batch of turkey feathers.

Roger turned his back on Stirling. "Hey, Kit," he said. "What's the matter with your boyfriend? He's awful quiet."

"Stirling is *not* my boyfriend," snapped Kit. "He and his mother *pay* to live at our house. They're *boarders*."

72

"Oh yeah!" Roger drawled. "That's right." He plopped himself down on the stool that Stirling had been using. Loudly and slowly, so that everyone could hear him, Roger said, "I heard that your family is so hard up you're running a boarding house now." He smirked. "And *you're* the maid."

"I am not!" Kit denied hotly. Of course, she *had* been feeling like a maid lately. But she'd never give Roger satisfaction by admitting it.

"That's not what I heard," Roger taunted. "Here's you." He pretended that his paintbrush was a maid's feather duster and he used it to brush some imaginary dust off his arms. Then he stood up, turned, and started to swagger away.

It was then that Kit saw the giant turkey feathers stuck to the seat of Roger's pants! Kit touched Ruthie's arm and pointed at Roger.

Ruthie chortled when she saw the feathers. "Hey, look, everybody!" she called out happily, pointing to Roger's bottom. "Look at Roger—Mr. Turkeypants!"

Everyone looked. The girls screamed with laughter and the boys whistled and clapped. "Hey, Turkeypants!" Ruthie hooted. "Gobble, gobble!"

Kit realized with surprise that Stirling must have sneaked the gluey feathers onto the stool just as Roger sat down so they'd stick to his pants when he stood up.

Roger also realized that Stirling was the one who'd tricked him. "You think you're pretty smart, don't you, Stirling?" he said furiously as he pulled off the gluey feathers. "Sticking your stupid turkey feathers on me. Well, at least *my* father hasn't flown the coop and disappeared like yours has!"

By now the whole class was gathered around Kit, Ruthie, Stirling, and Roger. They all looked at Stirling, waiting to hear what he'd say to Roger.

But Stirling didn't say anything, and his silence exasperated Kit. "For your information, birdbrain," she said to Roger, "Stirling's father sent him a letter from Chicago just a few days ago." She paused for impact. "And it had twenty dollars in it! His mother gave ten dollars to my mother."

Everyone gasped. *"Twenty dollars!"* they whispered in amazement.

"Well," sneered Roger. "That's good news for *your* family then, Kit, since your father doesn't have a job *or* any money. My father says your dad used

74

up all of his savings to pay the people who worked at his car dealership, which was stupid. No wonder no one will offer him a job."

"That's not true!" said Kit, outraged. "My father has job interviews all the time. Almost every day he has big, fancy lunches and meetings about jobs. He'll get one any day now. He said so."

"No, he won't," said Roger. "Nobody wants your father."

With that, Roger shoved his armful of sticky turkey feathers at Kit, who shoved them right back. Kit was so angry and shoved so hard that Roger staggered backward, lost his balance, and fell against a ladder that had a bucket of white paint on it. Everyone shrieked in horror and delight as the can fell over, splattering white paint on the backdrop and clonking Roger on the head! White paint spilled over Roger's hair and face and shoulders and back and arms. It ran in rivers down Roger, striping his legs and his socks and pooling into white puddles around his shoes.

"Arrgghh!" Roger roared. He swiped his hand across his face to clear the paint out of his eyes and then lunged for Kit.

*Everyone shrieked in horror and delight as the can fell over, splattering
white paint on the backdrop and clonking Roger on the head!*

But at that very instant, Mr. Fisher appeared. "Stop!" he shouted.

Roger stopped. Everyone was quiet.

Mr. Fisher frowned as he surveyed the white mess. "Who's responsible for this?" he demanded.

"Not me!" said Roger. "Stirling started it. He stuck feathers on me. And then Ruthie called me Mr. Tur—a stupid name—and Kit shoved me into the ladder. *They* did it, not me. They—"

Mr. Fisher held up his hand. "Quiet," he said. "Roger, go to the boys' room and clean yourself up. Boys and girls, I want you to go back to the classroom and sit silently at your desks. Kit, Ruthie, and Stirling, you three stay here. I want to talk to you."

Roger scuttled past Kit on his way out. "*Now* you're going to get it," he hissed at her, sounding pleased. "*Now* you'll be sorry!"

READ ALL OF KIT'S STORIES,
available at bookstores and *www.americangirl.com.*

MEET KIT • An American Girl
Kit Kittredge and her family get news that
turns their household upside down.

KIT LEARNS A LESSON • A School Story
It's Thanksgiving, and Kit learns a surprising
lesson about being thankful.

KIT'S SURPRISE • A Christmas Story
The Kittredges may lose their house.
Can Kit still find a way to make Christmas
merry and bright for her family?

HAPPY BIRTHDAY, KIT! • A Springtime Story
Kit loves Aunt Millie's thrifty ideas—until Aunt Millie
plans a pinch-penny party and invites Kit's whole class.

KIT SAVES THE DAY • A Summer Story
Kit's curiosity and longing for adventure
lead her to unexpected places—and into trouble!

CHANGES FOR KIT • A Winter Story
Kit writes a letter that brings changes and
new hope—in spite of the hard times.

◆

WELCOME TO KIT'S WORLD • 1934
American history is lavishly portrayed
with photographs, illustrations, and
excerpts from real girls' letters and diaries.